45 RPM
Record Company sleeves
Identification & Price Guide

Compiled By

Shelby Scott

Every effort has been made by the author and publisher of this book to provide accurate information on the subject matter of this book. Even though the information in this book has been carefully checked and researched, the author and publisher disclaim any responsibility for any errors and or omissions.

No portion of this book may be reproduced in any form or by any means, electronic or mechanical, including recording, photocopying, or by any storage or retrieval system, without the written permission from the author and publisher.

This book is dedicated to my wife Eileen, my best friend, the love of my life, a wonderful woman with a beautiful soul and a giving heart.

Acknowledgments

I would like to express my appreciation to all the people who contributed their time, assistance, research and their knowledge throughout the process of creating this reference guide. Their assistance has been indispensable.

A special acknowledgement goes to 45-Sleeves.com whose website helped in assisting with this book. I encourage all readers to visit this website.

45-sleeves.com

Table of Contents

INTRODUCTION

Valuation of Record Company Sleeves

The prices in this guide are just estimates of what a Record Company Sleeve would sell for in any transaction between a knowledgeable buyer and seller.

Prices listed in this book are also determined by the Rarity of the sleeve, the Design of the sleeve, the Condition of the sleeve and the record company name, but ultimately what the collector would pay for it. That's where this guide comes in it is there only as a "guide". The prices and range of prices printed in this book are not written in stone.

Prices listed are for NM (Near Mint) sleeves. The range for example $6 - $8 is

an estimation of what the sleeve would sell for on the low end or top end. Some of the prices may be too low or too high for some collectors or dealers but after researching and consulting many knowledgeable dealers and collectors this is whay was determined.

Grading of Record Company Sleeves

Record Company Sleeves in lesser condition than Near Mint are worth just a fraction of the Near Mint prices listed here.

NM Sleeves should not have any noticeable defects such as creases, small tears, bent corners, wrinkles etc.

VG+ sleeves should have only minor wear such as a small crease, seam wear, a very small split at the bottom seam.

VG Sleeves will have more creasing, seam splits possibly writing on it.

Sleeves not listed;

Not all sleeves are listed in this book. There are so many different record companies who never manufactured a company sleeve but instead used a plain brown sleeve.

There are smaller companies out there that did make a sleeve but only a few were made and I didn't have access to them.

This book only covers sleeves from 1950 through 1969. Please be aware that the same sleeve that was used for a 1969 released record may also continue into the 1970's.

About the book;

This book is set up in alphabetical order. The index at the back of the book is a great tool to use. You will find that many different labels used the same sleeve such in the case of Atlantic – Atco who distributed many different records.

The pictures of sleeves are all in color. Any additional information about a sleeve is listed either just below the sleeve name or below the sleeve grade. There is no way for us to include all information in this book. If you want more information such as what label went with what sleeve you can go to the following website;

45-Sleeves.com

How to Use This Book;

Front / Back – This is used when the sleeve has the same design on both the front and back

If there is a different design on the back of the sleeve it will have two photos one of the photos will have Front printed below it and the next photo will have back printed below it.

The sleeves pictured will also have a date or date range listed below it, this information was gathered from many different sources. Some may have Late 1960's printed, that's because it was used for several years in the late 1960's. Some sleeves actually have the date printed below it. This was used only when we were confident of the year it was issued.

When a sleeve is multiple times throughout several years or just for a different genre of music there will be different designs. The first sleeve will be listed as *Style "A"* the second *Style "B"* etc.

Example;

Style "A" Has Circle logo in top left corner.
1966 – 1967
$2 - $4

Style "B" has "Square" logo at top left corner. 1967 – 1969
$2 - $4

Grading:

All prices in this book are based on NM (Near Mint) condition sleeves.

Grading record company sleeves is the same as grading picture sleeves.

Goldmine Standards for grading picture sleeves is should be used.

Near Mint (NM) – No seam splits, no creases or ring wear.

This book in no way covers all record company sleeves.

Many references have been consulted in order to complete this guide. However, I am sure that errors and omissions are present, further research and help from collectors will be is necessary and a 2nd addition will most likely be printed.

.

A&M

Founded by Herb Alpert and Jerry Moss – This label continued into the 1980's

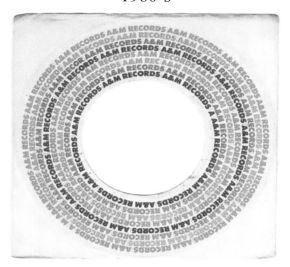

Style "A" 1960 – 1969

$2 - $4

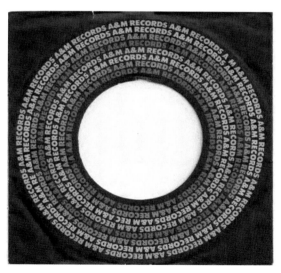

Style "B" 1969 – 1972

$2 - $4

ABC

Originally "ABC – Paramount" records the name changed to "ABC" in 1966

Style "A" Has Circle logo in top left corner. 1966 – 1967

$2 - $4

Style "B" has "Square" logo at top left corner. 1967 – 1969

$2 - $4

ABC Paramount

Started in 1955 and changed its name to "ABC" in 1966

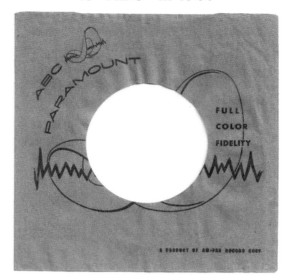

Style "A" 1955 – 1958

$3 - $5

This sleeve comes in several different styles.

Type A – Purple print brown sleeve

Type B – Purple print green sleeve

Type C – Purple print off white and white sleeve

Although the purple print is more common some sleeves may come with black print – This does not affect the value.

ABC Paramount

Front

Style "B" – 1958 – 1962

$3 - $5

ABC Paramount

Back

Style "B" Style "A" – 1958 – 1962

The back has several different listings of recording stars printed on this side throughout the years of production. This does not affect the value.

ABC Paramount

Back

Style "B" Style "B" – 1958 – 1962

Notice the circles are plain white. This does not affect the value.

ABC Paramount

Back

Style "C" – 1960 – 1962

"A Stereo Record"

ABC Paramount

Front

Style "C" – 1960 – 1962

"A Stereo Record"

$10 - $15

ABC Paramount

Front / Back

Style "D" – 1962 – 1966

Front and Back are the same.

This sleeve comes with a brown and also a white background which does not affect value.

$3 - $5

ABC Paramount

Front / Back

Style "E" – 1956 – 1961?

$3 - $5

Front and Back are the same style with different artists listed.

This sleeve comes with a red and also a grey background which does not affect value.

ABC Paramount

Front

Style "F" – 1957 – 1962?

$6 - $8

This sleeve is a white background with red print and used exclusively for Promotional records.

Accent

Front / Back

Circa 1964

$4 - $6

ACE

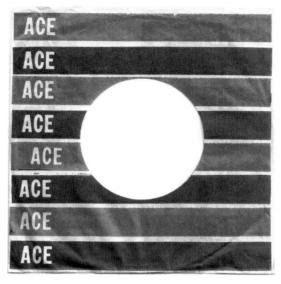

Front
Style "A" 1959 – 1963
$8 - $10

ACE

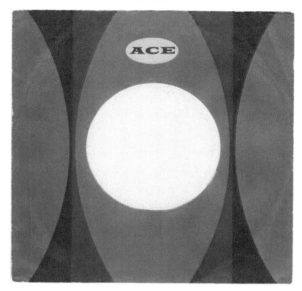

Front / Back
Style "B" 1963
$6 - $8

Back
Style "A"
1959 – 1963

ACE - HI

Front
Back is plain brown sleeve
Issued 1 year 1952/53
$10- $15

ACME

Front

Style "A" Back is plain brown sleeve

Kentucky Label – 1956 - 1959

$10 - $15

Style "B" This sleeve also comes with a side opening similarly valued

ACME

Front / Back

New York label 1957/58

$6 - $8

ACTA

A division of "DOT" Records

Front / Back

1967 – 1969 - $2 - $3

AGP

Front / Back

Style "A" 1968 -1969

$2 - $4

AGP was distributed by "Bell" Records. See "BELL"

AGP

Front / Back

Sltyle "B" 1969 / 70

$2 - $4

AGP was distributed by "Bell"
Records. See "BELL"

ALADDIN

Front

Style "A" 1951? / 1958

$20 - $25

ALADDIN

Back

Style "A" 1951? / 1958

ALADDIN

Front

Style "B" 1958 / 1961

$4 - $6

This sleeve is blue with white
background and also comes red with
brown background

ALADDIN

Back

Style "B" 1958 / 1961

Notice the five heads below center of hole

ALADDIN

Back

Style "C" 1961

Notice the five heads below center of hole

ALADDIN

Front

Style "C" 1961

$4 - $6

Red with brown background, notice the large "Head" (Thurston Harris) on the right side of sleeve.

ALLIED RECORDS

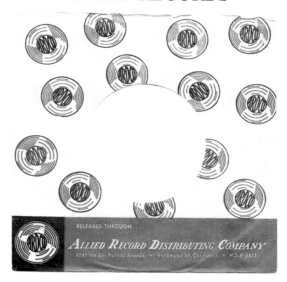

Front / Back
1959 – 1961
$8 - $10

Allied Records was a distributor. It distributed the following record labels with this one sleeve.

- Silver
- Crest
- Dico
- Milestone
- Domino
- Swingin'
- Caplehart

ALMA

Front / Back
Circa 1953
$10 - $12

ALSTON
Distributed by "Atlantic – Atco"

Front / Back
Circa 1968 – 1970
$3 - $5

Amaret

Front / Back

Green sleeve 1969

$8- $10

AMERICAN ARTS

Front / Back

Red, White and Blue sleeve

1964/65

$8 - $10

AMY

Front / Back

1960 – 1969

$2 - $4

"Amy" was distributed by "Bell" Records. See "BELL"

APPLE

Front / Back

1968 / 69

$2 - $4

APT

Front

Style "A" 1958/59

$4 - $6

Color is red print and stars with white/ off white background. Back of sleeve is missing red line at the top.

Front / Back

Style "B" 1959/60 – 1966

$4 - $6

ARIEL Records
(Distributed by Musicor)

Front / Back

Circa 1968

$4 - $6

ARROW

Front / Back

Circa 1956/57 – Brown Sleeve

$10 - $15

ARROW

Front / Back

Circa 1957/58 – White Sleeve

$10 - $15

ASCOT

Front / Back

Circa 1962 – 1967

$4 - $6

Sleeve came in off white and light green.

ATCO

Front / Back

Style "A"

1955 – 1959

$4 - $6

Sleeves are white with yellow and black print. (Some sleeves have brown background)

ATCO

Front / Back

Style "B"

1969

$3 - $5

ATLANTIC

Front

Style "A" brown sleeve

1951 – 1953

$10 - $15

ATLANTIC

Style "A" Back

Artists;

Ruth Brown

The Cardinals

Joe Turner

The Clovers

Joe Morris

ATLANTIC

Style "B" Back

1953 - 1960

$10 - $15

Same front as previous listing

Artists;

Joe Turner

La Vern Baker

Clyde McPhatter and the Drifters
Ruth Brown

The Clovers

Ray Charles

ATLANTIC

Front / Back

Style "C" (Black Stripes, top filled with black)

Circa 1960 / 61

$8 - $10

Front / Back

Style "D" (Black Stripes, top filled with white with black ink)

This sleeve was also produced with purple stripes and red print similarly valued

Circa 1962 - 1964

$6- $8

ATLANTIC

Front / Back

Style "E" 1965 – 1969

$3 - $5

Atlantic Atco Group

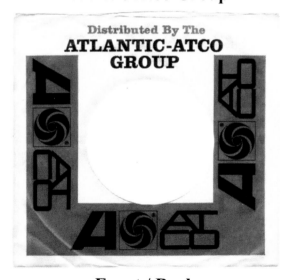

Front / Back

Style "A"

1965 – 1969

$3 - $5

The Atlantic and Atco labels were never distributed in these sleeves only subsidiary labels

Atlantic Atco Group

Front / Back

Style "B" 1969 -7?

$3 - $5

The Atlantic and Atco labels were never distributed in these sleeves only subsidiary labels.

AVCO

Front / Back

1968 / 69

$3 - $5

AVA

Front / Back

1962 – 1965

$10 - $15

BALLY

Front

1956 – 1957

$6 - $8

Back

BELL

Front / Back

Style "A" / Issued from 1953 – 196?

$2 - $3 - Light Grey / Grey

Front / Back

Style "B" / Issued from 1953 – 196?

$2 - $3

Four Colors;

- **Pink**
- **Orange**
- **Blue**
- **Green**

BELL

Front / Back

Style "C" 1960 / 69

1960 – 1969

$2 - $4

Several shades of color exist - same value

Front / Back

Style "B" 1969 / 70

$2 - $4

Several shades of color exist same value.

BETHLEHEM

Front / Back

Style "A"

1954 - 1958

New York address

$15 - $20

Front / Back

Style "B"

1958 - 1962

$8- $12

BETHLEHEM

Front / Back

Style "C"

1962 – 196?

$8- $12

BIG WAY RECORDS

Distributed by Boyd

Front / Back

1969

$10 - $15

BIG TOP

Front / Back

1958 – 196?

$6 - $8

BLUE

Distributed by Atlantic-Atco

Front / Back

1969 -7?

$3 - $5

BLUE NOTE

Front / Back

1956 – 196?

$6 - $8

BLUE ROCK

Front / Back

1968 – 1969?

$4 - $6

BLUE ROCK

Front / Back

1964 – 1967?

$4 - $6

BLUE THUMB
Distributed by ABC Records

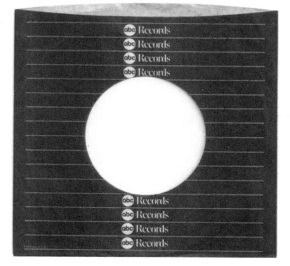

Front / Back

1969 – 197?

$2 - $4

BLUESWAY
Distributed by ABC Records

Front / Back
1967 – 1969
$4 - $6

BROADMOOR
Distributed By Dover Records

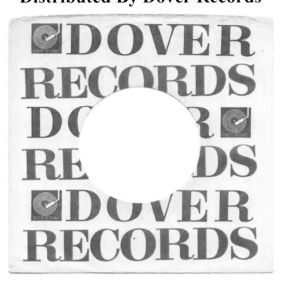

Front / Back
1967 / 68
$3 - $5

BOOM
Distributed By ABC Paramount

Front / Back
1966
$20 - $25

BROADWAY

Front / Back
Style "A"
Early 1950's
$8 - $10

B

BROADWAY

Front / Back
Style "B"
Early 1950's
$8 - $10

BRUNSWICK

Front / Back
Style "A"
1949 - 1956
$4 - $6

BROTHER
Distributed By Capitol Records

Front / Back
1967 - 1969
$2- $4

Front
Style "B"
1957 - 1960
$4 - $6

BRUNSWICK

Back
Style "B"
1957 - 1960

BRUNSWICK

Back
Style "C"
1960 / 61

BRUNSWICK

Front
Style "C"
1960 / 61
$4 - $6

BRUNSWICK

Front
Style "D"
1961 – 1964
$4 - $6

BRUNSWICK

Back

Style "D"

1961 – 1964

$4 - $6

BRUNSWICK

Back

Style "E"

1964 – 1969

$3 - $5

BRUNSWICK

Front

Style "E"

1964 – 1969

$3 - $5

BUDDAH

Front / Back

1967 – 1969

$3 - $5

BUENA VISTA

Front / Back

1963 – 1967

$3 - $5

Buena Vista was started in 1959 we are unsure of the correct company sleeve. Any help with this would be appreciated.

BUNKY

Distributed By Scepter Records

Front / Back

1967 – 1969

$4 - $6

BURDETTE

Affiliated with Jerden Records

Front / Back

1968 – 1969

$4 - $6

CADENCE

Front (Back is plain)

Style "A"

1953 / 54

$15 - $20

CADENCE

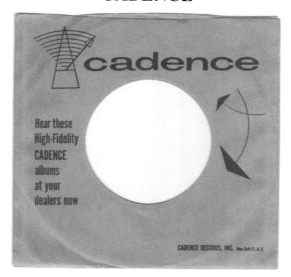

Front
Style "B"
Early 1950"s
$4 - $6

CADENCE

Front
Style "C"
Mid to Late 1950"s
$4 - $6

Back
Style "B"
Early 1950"s

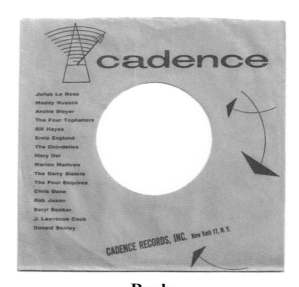

Back
Style "C"
Mid to Late 1950"s

CADENCE

Front
Style "D"
Early 1960's
$3 - $5

Back
Style "D"
Early 1960's

CADET

Front / Back
Style "A":
Mid 1960's
$4 - $6

CADET

Front / Back
Style "B":
Mid 1960's
$2 - $4

CADET

Front / Back
Style "C":
Late 1960's
$2 - $4

CALENDAR

Front / Back
Style "A"
Late 1960's
$2 - $4

CADET CONCEPT

Front / Back
Late 1960's
$2 - $4

CALENDAR

Front / Back
Style "B"
Late 1960's
$2 - $4

C

CANADIAN AMERICAN

Front / Back

Late 1950's – 1968

$4 - $6

CAPITOL

Front

Style "A"

1949 – 1950

$25 - $30

Capitol used a flap the first year it
manufactured 45's.

CAPITOL

Back

Style "A"

1949 – 1950

$25 - $30

CAPITOL

Front

Style "B"

Early 1950's

$3 - $5

CAPITOL

Back
Style "B"
Early 1950's
$3 - $5

CAPITOL

Front / Back
Style "C"
Mid / Late 1950's
$3 - $5

CAPITOL

Front / Back
Style "C"
Early 1950's
$3 - $5

CAPITOL

Front / Back
Style "D"
Mid / Late 1950's
$4 - $6

CAPITOL

Front / Back

Style "E"

Mid / Late 1950's

$3 - $5

CAPITOL

Front / Back

Style "G"

Mid / Late 1950's

$6- $8

CAPITOL

Front / Back

Style "F"

Mid / Late 1950's

$6- $8

CAPITOL

Front / Back

Style "H"

Mid 1950's

$2- $4

CAPITOL

Front
Style "I"
Mid 1950's
$3- $5

CAPITOL

Front / Back
Style "J"
Mid / Late 1950's
$3- $5

Back
Style "I"
Mid 1950's
$3- $5

CAPITOL

Front
Style "K"
Late 1950's
$3- $5

CAPITOL

Back
Style "K"
Late 1950's
$3 - $5

CAPITOL

Front / Back
Style "M"
Early 1960's
$2 - $4

CAPITOL

Front / Back
Style "L"
Late 1950's / Early 1960's
$3 - $5

CAPITOL

Front / Back
Style "N"
Early / Mid 1960's
$8 - $10

CAPITOL

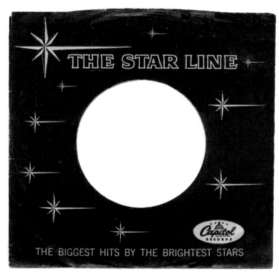

Front / Back
Style "O"
Late 1960's
$2 - $4

CAPITOL STARLINE

Back
Style "A"
Late 1950's – Mid 1960's
$3 - $5

CAPITOL STARLINE

Front
Style "A"
Late 1950's – Mid 1960's
$3 - $5

CAPITOL STARLINE

Front
Style "B"
Mid – Late 1960's
$3 - $5

CAPITOL STARLINE

Back

Style "B"

Mid – Late 1960's

$3 - $5

CAPRICON

Distributed By Atlantic – Atco

Front / Back

1969 -7?

$3 - $5

CAPITOL STARLINE

Front / Back

Style "C"

Late 1960's

$2 - $4

CARLTON

Front / Back

Style "A"

Late 1950's / Early 1960's

$6 - $8

Several other colors

CARLTON

Front / Back
Style "B"
Early / Mid 1960's
$10 - $15

CENTAUR

Distributed by Cameo - Parkway

Front / Back
1966 – 1967
$4 - $6

CASTLE

Front / Back
1958
$10 - $15

CENTURY

Front / Back
Late 1960's
$6 - $8

CHALLENGE

Front / Back

1958 – 1965

$8 - $10

CHALLENGE

Front / Back

Late 1960's

$6 - $8

CHALLENGE

Front / Back

Mid 1960's

$6 - $8

CHANCELLOR

Front / Back

1959 – Early 1960's

$4 - $6

CHANCELLOR

Front
Mid 1960's
$8 - $10

CHANCELLOR

Back
Mid 1960's
$8 - $10

CHAPTER ONE
Distributed by London Records

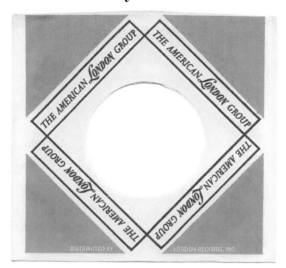

Front / Back
Late 1960's
$3 - $5

CHART

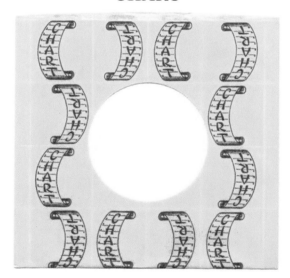

Front / Back
1969
$8 - $10

CHECKER
Distributed by Chess Records

Front / Back
Style "A":
Mid 1960's
$2 - $4

CHESS

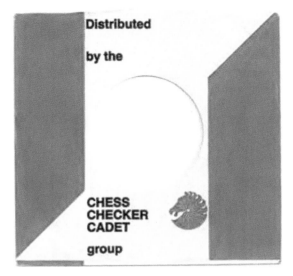

Front / Back
Style "A":
Mid 1960's
$2 - $4

CHECKER
Distributed by Chess Records

Front / Back
Style "B":
Mid / Late 1960's
$2 - $4

CHESS

Front / Back
Style "B":
Mid / Late 1960's
$2 - $4

C

CHISA

Front / Back

Late 1960's

$4 - $6

CHOREO

Front / Back

Early 1960's

$8 - $10

CIRCA

Consolidated International Record Company

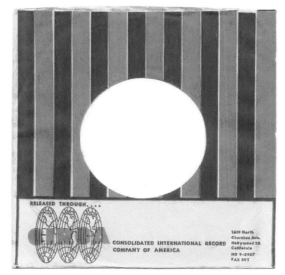

Front / Back

Early 1960's

$8 - $10

Circa distributed the following labels;

Amazon

Crest

Gambit

Invicta

Milestone

Tempe

CLASS

Front / Back
Style "A"
Late 1950's – Early 1960's
$6 - $8

CLEF

Front / Back
1952 – 1956
$8 - $10

CLASS

Front / Back
Style "B"
Early 1960's – Mid 1960's
$6 - $8

CLOCK

Front
Style "A"
1959 – 1961
$10 - $15

CLOCK

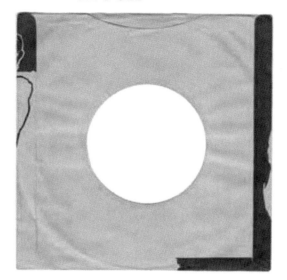

Back
Style "A"
1959 – 1961

CLOCK

Front / Back
Style "B"
Early 1960's
$6 - $8

CLOCK
Distributed by Mercury Records

Front / Back
Style "C"
Early 1960's
$6 - $8

COBBLESTONE
Subsidiary of Buddah Records

Front / Back
Late 1960's
$3 - $5

COED

Front / Back
Style "A"
Late 1950's – Early 1960's
$8 - $10

COLGEMS

Front b/ Back
Late 1960's
$3 - $5

COED

Front / Back
Style "B"
Early 1960's – Mid 1960's
$8 - $10

COLOSSUS

Front / Back
1969
$8 - $10

COLPIX

Front / Back
Style "A"
Late 1950's – Early 1960's
$6 - $8

COLUMBIA

Front / Back
Style "A"
Early 1950's – Mid 1950's
$3 -$5

COLPIX

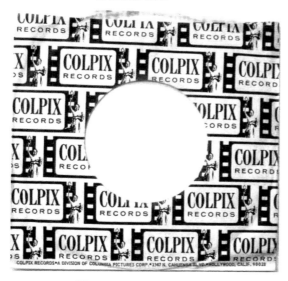

Front / Back
Style "B"
Early 1960's – Mid 1960's
$6 - $8

COLUMBIA

Front
Style "B"
Mid 1950's
$3 -$5

COLUMBIA

Back
Style "B"
Mid 1950's
$3 -$5

COLUMBIA

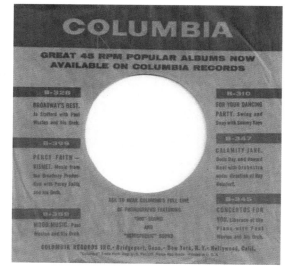

Front / Back
Style "D"
Mid 1950's
$3 -$5

COLUMBIA

Front / Back
Style "C"
Mid 1950's
$3 -$5

COLUMBIA

Front / Back
Style "E"
Mid 1950's
$3 -$5

COLUMBIA

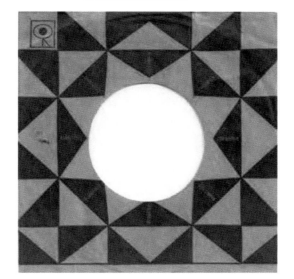

Front / Back

Style "F"

Mid 1950's

$3 - $5

COLMBIA

Front / Back

Style "H"

Late 1950's – Early 1960's

$3 - $5

Also comes in off white, brown, light brown and various shades of each.

COLUMBIA

Front / Back

Style "G"

Mid – Late 1950's

$3 - $5

COLUMBIA

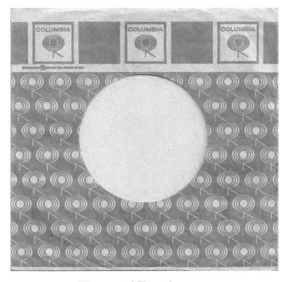

Front / Back

Style "I"

Early 1960's

$3 - $5

COLUMBIA

Front / Back

Style "J"

Mid - Late 1960's

$2 - $4

This sleeve also came in a
variety of colors all similarly
valued

COLUMBIA PRICELESS EDITIONS

Front (Back is plain)

1949 – 1950

$8 - $10

COLUMBIA

Front / Back

Style "K"

Late 1960's

$2 - $4

COMMONWEALTH UNITED

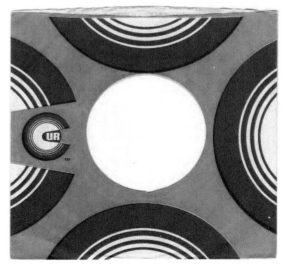

Front / Back

Late 1960's

$4 - $6

CONTINENTAL

Front / Back
Circa 1950's
$10 - $15

CORAL

Front / Back
Style "A"
Early – Late 1950's
$3 - $5

CORAL

Front / Back
Style "B"
(Notice the "45" middle left)
Circa 1950's
$3 - $5

CORAL

Front
Style "C"
Late 1950's
$6 - $8

CORAL

Back
Style "C"
Late 1950's
$6 - $8

CORAL

Back
Style "D"
Late 1950's
$3 - $5

CORAL

Front
Style "D"
Late 1950's
$3 - $5

CORAL

Front /Back
Style "E"
Late 1950's
$3 - $5

C

CORAL

Front
Style "F"
Early 1960's
$3 - $5

CORAL

Front
Style "G"
Early – Mid 1960's
$3 - $5

CORAL

Back
Style "F"
Early 1960's
$3 - $5

CORAL

Back
Style "G"
Early – Mid 1960's
$3 - $5

CORAL

Front

Style "H"

Mid 1960's

$3 - $5

CORAL

Front

Style "I"

Late 1960's

$3 - $5

CORAL

Back

Style "H"

Mid 1960's

$3 - $5

CORAL

Back

Style "I"

Late 1960's

$3 - $5

COTILLION
Distributed by Atlantic - Atco

Front / Back

Style "A"

Late 1960's

$3 - $5

COTILLION

Front / Back

Style "C"

Circa 1969'

$3 - $5

COTILLION

Front / Back

Style "B"

Circa 68' / 69'

$3 - $5

COUNTRY & WESTERN HITS

Front / Back

Style "A"

Early 1960's

$4 - $6

COUNTRY & WESTERN HITS

Front / Back

Style "B"

Early – Mid 1960's

$4 - $6

COUNTRY & WESTERN HITS

Front / Back

Style "D"

Mid 1960's

$4 - $6

COUNTRY & WESTERN HITS

Front / Back

Style "C"

Mid – Late 1960's

$4 - $6

COUNTRY & WESTERN HITS

Front / Back

Style "E"

Mid 1960's

$4 - $6

CRAZY HORSE
Subsidiary of Capitol Records

Front / Back
Late 1960's
$2 - $4

CREST

Front (Back is plain)
Style "A"
Late 1950's
$8 - $10

CREAM

Front / Back
Late 1960's
$4 - $6

CREST
Distributed by Allied Records

Front / Back
Style "B"
1959 – 1961
$8 - $10

CREST

Distributed by Consolidated International Records

Front / Back

Style "C"

Early 1960's

$8 - $10

CROSBY

Front / Back

Early 1960's

$8 - $10

CREWE

Front / Back

Late 1960's

$3 - $5

Crown

Front / Back

Mid 1950's

$8 - $10

CRYSTALETTE

Front (Back is plain)
Style "A"
Early 1950's
$10 - $15

CTI
Distributed by A&M Records

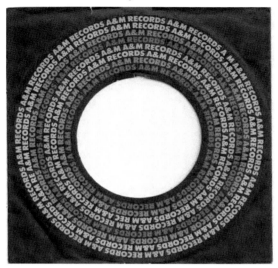

Front /Back
Late 1960's
$2 - $4

CRYSTALETTE

Front / Back
Style "B"
Late 1950's
$10 - $15

CUB

Front / Back
Late 1950's – Early 1960's
$4 -$6

CUCA

Front / Back
Early 1960's
$10 - $15

A blue sleeve also exists, similar value

DANA

Front / Back
1950's
$3 - $5

CURTOM

Front / Back
Late 1960's
$3 - $5

DATE

Front / Back
Style "A"
Late 1950's
$8 - $10
DATE

Front / Back
Style "B"
Mid 1960's
$8 - $10

DCP

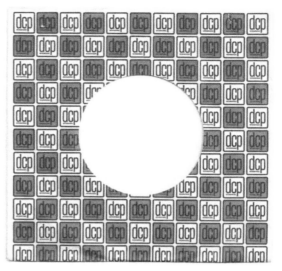

Front / Back
Mid 1960's
$4 - $8

DATE

Front / Back
Style "C"
Late 1960's
$3 - $5

DELUXE

Front / Back
Style "A"
Early - Mid 1950's
$4 - $6

DELUXE

Front / Back
Style "B"
Late1950's
$8 - $12

DEARBORN

Front / Back
1965 – 1969
$10 - $15

DELUXE

Front / Back
Style "C"
1958 - 1962
$8- $12

DECCA

Front / Back
Style "A"
Early 1950's
$4 - $6

DECCA

Front
Style "B"
Early 1950's
$3 - $5

DECCA

Front
Style "C"
Early 1950's
$3 - $5

DECCA

Back
Style "B"
Early 1950's
$3 - $5

DECCA

Back
Style "C"
Early 1950's
$3 - $5

DECCA

Front
Style "D"
Early 1950's
$3 - $5

DECCA

Front / Back
Style "E"
Mid 1950's
$3 - $5

DECCA

Back
Style "D"
Early 1950's
$3 - $5

DECCA

Front (Back is Plain)
Style "F"
Mid 1950's
$4 - $6

DECCA

Front
Style "G"
Late 1950's
$3 - $5

Front
Style "H"
Late 1950's
$4 - $6

DECCA

Back
Style "G"
Late 1950's
$3 - $5

DECCA

Back
Style "H"
Late 1950's
$4 - $6

DECCA

DECCA

Front
Style "I"
Early 1960's
$3 - $5

DECCA

Front
Style "J"
Early - Mid 1960's
$3 - $5

DECCA

Back
Style "I"
Early 1960's
$3 - $5

DECCA

Front
Style "K"
Mid 1960's
$2 - $4

DECCA

Back
Style "K"
Mid 1960's
$2 - $4

DECCA

Back
Style "L"
Mid 1960's
$2 - $4

DECCA

Front
Style "L"
Mid 1960's
$2 - $4

DECCA

Front
Style "M"
Mid – Late 1960's
$2 - $4

DECCA

Back
Style "M"
Mid – Late 1960's
$2 - $4

DECCA

Back
Style "N"
Mid – Late 1960's
$2 - $4

DECCA

Front
Style "N"
Mid – Late 1960's
$2 - $4

DECCA

Front
Style "O"
Late 1960's
$2 - $4

DECCA

Back
Style "O"
Late 1960's
$2 - $4

DERAM

Front / Back
Style "B"
Late 1960's
$3 - $5

DERAM

Front / Back
Style "A"
Circa 1966 / 67
$3 - $5

DERBY

Front / Back
Early – Mid 1950's
$10 - $12

DIAMOND

Front / Back
Circa 1950's
$15 - $20

DIXIE OLDIES

Subsidiary of Good Time Jazz

Front / Back
Mid 1960's
$4 - $6

DIAMOND

Front / Back
Circa 1960's
$6 - $8

DJM

Front / Back
1969
$4 - $6

DOLTON
A Division of Liberty Records

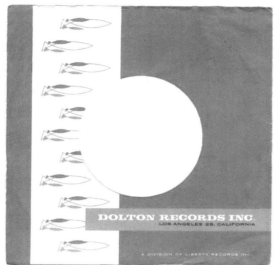

Front / Back

Early 1960's

$8 - $10

DOLTON

Front / Back

1966 – 67'

$6 - $8

DOLTON

Front / Back

Mid 1960's

$6 - $8

DOOTO

Front / Back

Late 50's – Early 60's

$15 $20

DOT

Front / Back
Style "A"
Early – Mid 1950's
$10 - $15

DOT

Back
Style "B"
Early 1950's
$10 - $15

DOT

Front
Style "B"
Early 1950's
$10 - $15

DOT

Front
Style "C"
Mid 1950's
$4 - $6

DOT

Back

Style "C"

Mid 1950's

$4 - $6

DOT

Front / Back

Style "D"

Mid – Late 1950's

$2 - $4

Many different variations do exist, such as color differences for both the sleeve and the print.

DOT

Front / Back

Style "D"

Mid 1950's

$4 - $6

DOT

Front / Back

Style "E"

Early 1960's

$3 - $5

DOT

Front (Different Back)

Style "F"

Early – Mid 1960's

$2 - $4

This type of sleeve was produced with at least 16 show different layouts of different pictures.

DOT

Front / Back

Style "G"

Circa 1964 - 1968

$3 $5

DOT

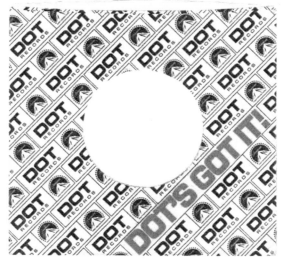

Front / Back

Style "H"

1968 – 69'

$2 - $4

DOUBLETALK

Distributed Through Nashboro

Front / Back

Circa 1969 $3 - $5

DUKE

Front / Back

Circa 1960's

$6 - $8

DUNHILL

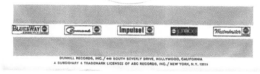

Front / Back

Style "B"

Circa 1969

$2 - $4

DUNHILL

Front / Back

Style "A"

1965 – 1969

$2 - $4

DUNWICH

Distributed by Atlantic - Atco

Front / Back

Mid 1960's

$3 - $5

DYNASTY

Front / Back

Circa early 1960's

$15 - $20

DYNOVOICE

Front / Back

Style "B"

Circa 1965 – 1966

$3 - $5

DYNOVOICE (VOX)

Front / Back

Style "A"

Circa 1965

$10 - $12

Dynovox changed its name to
Dynovoice in 1965

DYNOVOICE

Front / Back

Style "C"

Circa 1967

$3 - $5

DYNOVOICE

Front / Back
Style "D"
Late 1960's
$3 - $5

ELF
Distributed by Bell

Front / Back
Mid – Late 1960's
$2 - $4

ELEKTRA

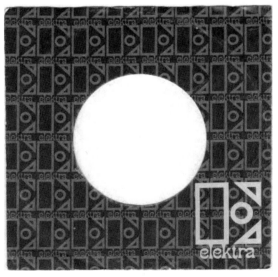

Front / Back
Mid – Late 1960's
$3 - $5

END

Front / Back
Style "A"
1957 – 1963
$6 - $8

END

Front / Back
Style "B"
1963 - 1964
$3 - $5

EPIC

Front
Style "A"
Circa 1953
$3 - $5

ENSIGN
Distributed by Mercury

Front / Back
Early 1960's
$6 - $8

EPIC

Back
Style "A"
Circa 1953/54
$3 - $5

There were several styles listing
different artists, similarly valued.

EPIC

Front / Back

Style "B"

Mid 1950's

$3 - $5

EPIC

Front / Back

Style "D"

Mid 1950's – Early 1960's

$3 - $5

(Note printing is no longer in the top left corner)

EPIC

Front / Back

Style "C"

Mid 1950's

$3 - $5

(Note printing in the top left corner)

EPIC

Front / Back

Style "E"

From 1961 – 1965 there were several different color sleeves and print.

$3 - $5

EPIC

Front / Back
Style "F"
Circa 1965 – 1968
$3 - $5

EQUINOX

Front / Back
1967 – 1968
$10 - $15

EPIC

Front / Back
Style "G"
Circa 1968 – 7?
$3 - $5

ERA

Front / Back
Style "A"
Mid – Late 1950's
$8 - $10

ERA

Front / Back
Style "B"
Early 1960's
$6 - $8

EVENT

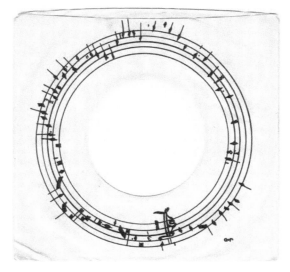

Front / Back
Late 1950's
$10 - $15

ERA

Front / Back
Style "C"
Circa 1960's
$3 - $5

EVEREST

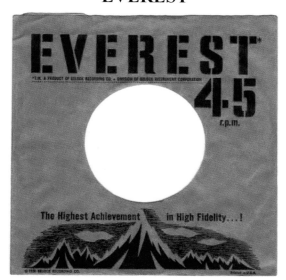

Front / Back
Style "A"
Late 1950's
$15 - $20

EVEREST

Front / Back

Style "B"

Circa 1960's

$4 - $6

This style of sleeve came in several different color schemes throughout the years of production. All are similarly valued.

EXCELLO

Distributed by Nasboro

Front / Back

Late 1960's

$3 - $5

FAME

Distributed by Atlantic - Atco

Front / Back

Mid 1960's

$3 - $5

FARGO

Front (Back is plain)

Early 1960's

$10 - $15

FAVORITE

Front / Back

1954

$8 - $10

FEDERAL

Distributed by King Records

Front / Back

Style "B"

Late 1950's

$8 - $10

FEDERAL

Distributed by King Records

Front / Back

Style "A"

Mid 1950's

$8 - $10

FEDERAL

Distributed by King Records

Front / Back

Style "C"

Early 1960's

$8 - $12

FEDERAL
Distributed by King Records

Front / Back

Style "D"

Early – Mid 1960's

$4 - $6

FIRE

Front / Back

Style "A"

Early 1960's

$10 - $15

FILLMORE

Front / Back

1969

$4 - $6

FIRE

Front / Back

Style "B"

Early 1960's

$15 - $20

FLAIR

Front / Back

Mid 1950's

$10 - $15

FLASHBACK
Distributed By Bell Records

Front / Back

Mid 1960's

$4 - $6

FLAIR X

Front / Back

1956 – 1957

$20 - $25

FONTANA

Front / Back

Mid 1960's

$3 - $5

FORD

Front (Back is plain)

Early 1960's

$10 - $15

4 CORNERS

Front / Back

Mid 1960's

$3 - $5

FORWARD

Front / Back

Late 1960's

$6 - $8

49th STATE HAWAII

Front / Back

Circa 1950's

$20 - $25

FRATERNITY

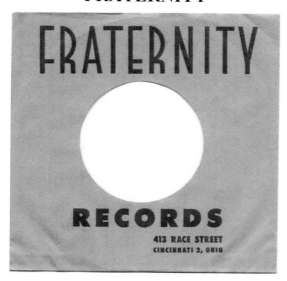

Front / Back

Mid 1950's

$6 - $8

FURY

Front / Back

Mid – Late 1960's

$8 - $10

FRATERNITY

Front / Back

Mid - Late 1950's

$6 - $8

GARDENA

Front / Back

Circa 1965

$8 - $10

GARRETT
Distributed by Soma Records

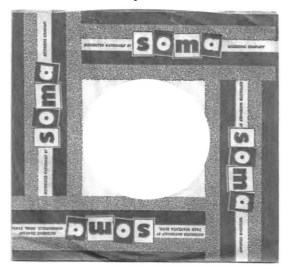

Front / Back
Mid 1960's
$6 - $8

GATEWAY

Front / Back
Style "B"
Late 1950's
$6 - $8

GATEWAY

Front / Back
Style "A"
Mid 1950's
$6 - $8

GEE

Front / Back
Style "A"
Mid 1950's
$6 - $8

GEE

Front / Back
Style "B"
Late 1950's
$6 - $8

GLOVER

Back
Mid 1960's
$3 - $5

GLOVER
Distributed by Roulette

Front
Mid 1960's
$3 - $5

GNP CRESCENDO

Front / Back
Style "A"
Early – Mid 1960s
$3 - $5

GNP CRESCENDO

Front / Back
Style "B"
Mid - Late 1960s
$3 - $5

GONE

Front
Early – Mid 1960's
$6 - $8

GOLDWAX
Distributed by Bell

Front / Back
Mid – Late 1960's
$2 - $4

GONE

Back
Early – Mid 1960's
$6 - $8

GORDY
Motown Records

Front / Back
Mid 1960's
$6 - $8

GROOVE

Front / Back
Style "A"
Mid - Late 1950's
$6 - $8

GREGAR
Distributed by Mercury

Front / Back
Late 1960's
$3 - $5

GROOVE

Front / Back
Style "B"
Early 1960's
$8 - $10

GROOVE

Front / Back
Style "C"
Mid 1960's
$8 - $10

GUARANTEED

Front / Back
Style "A"
Late 1950's – Early 1960's
$6 - $8

GRT

Front / Back
Late 1960's
$2 - $4

GUARANTEED

Front / Back
Style "B"
Early 1960's
$3 - $5

GWP

Front / Back

1969

$6 - $8

HANOVER

Front / Back

Early 1960's

$10 - $15

HANNA BARBERA RECORDS (HBR)

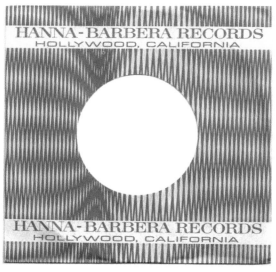

Front / Back

Mid 1960's

$4 - $6

HEADLINE

Front / Back

Late 1950's

$15 - $20

HEARTBEAT

Front (Back is plain)

Early 1960's

$15 - $20

HICKORY

Front / Back

Style "A"

Late 1950's

$10 - $12

Hi

Front / Back

Early 1960's

$4 - $6

HICKORY

Front / Back

Style "B"

1960's

$3 - $5

Several colors were available all are similarly valued.

HILLTOP

Front

Mid 1960's

$6 - $8

Hot Biscuit

Front / Back

Late 1960's

$3 - $5

HILLTOP

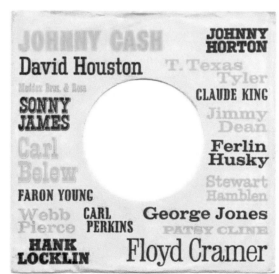

Back

Mid 1960's

$6 - $8

HOT WAX

Distributed by Buddah

Front / Back

1969

$3 - $5

IMMEDIATE

Front / Back
Late 1960's
$3 - $5

IMPERIAL

Front / Back
Style "B"
Early – Mid 1950's
$8 - $10

IMPERIAL

Front / Back
Style "A"
Early 1950's
$15 - $20

IMPERIAL

Front / Back
Style "C"
Late 1950's – Early 1960's
$3 - $5

IMPERIAL

Front
Style "D"
Early 1960's
$3 - $5

IMPERIAL

Front
Style "E"
Early – Mid 1960's
$3 - $5

IMPERIAL

Back
Style "D"
Early 1960's
$3 - $5

IMPERIAL

Back
Style "E"
Early – Mid 1960's
$3 - $5

IMPERIAL

Front / Back

Style "F"

Mid – Late 1960's

Several color combinations throughout production, all are similarly valued.

INTEGRA

Front (Back is plain)

Late 1960's

$3 - $5

INFINITY

Front / Back

Early 1960's

$15 - $20

INTREPID

Distributed by Mercury Records

Front / Back

Late 1960's

$# - $5

INVICTUS

Front / Back
1969
$3 - $5

JAMIE

Front / Back
Style "A"
Late 1950's – Early 1960's
$15 - $20

JAD

Front / Back
1968 – 1969
$4 - $6

JAMIE

Front / Back
Style "B"
Mid – Late 1960's
$6 - $8

JAMIE
Distributed by Jamie/Guyden

Front / Back

Style "C"

Late 1960's

$3 - $5

JANUS

Front / Back

Late 1960's

$3 - $5

JAN

Front (Back is plain)

1959

$10 - $15

JAY JAY

Front (Back is plain)

Style "A"

Circa 1950's

$20 - $25

JAY JAY

Front / Back
Style "B"
Circa 1960's
$8 - $10

JIN

Front / Back
Circa 1950's
$10 - $15

JEWEL

Front / Back
Circa 1960s
$6 - $8

JONES

Front / Back
Circa Late 1950's
$20 - $25

JOSIE
The Jubilee Group

Front / Back
Circa 1960's
$6 - $8

JUBILEE

Front / Back
Style "A"
Circa 1950's
$6 - $8

JOY

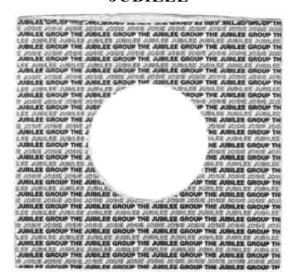

Front / Back
Circa Late 1950's Early 1960's
$10 - $15

JUBILEE

Front / Back
Circa 1960's
$6 - $8

K & H

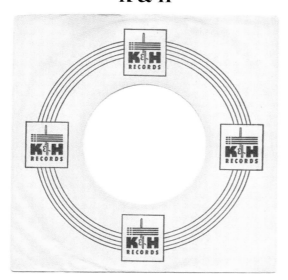

Front / Back
Early 1960's
$6 - $8

KAPP

Front
Style "B"
Early 1960's
$3 - $5

KAPP

Front / Back
Style "A"
Mid – Late 1950's
$6 - $8

KAPP

Back
Style "B"
Early 1960's
$3 - $5

KAPP

Front

Style "C"

Early 1960's

$4 - $6

KAPP

Front / Back

Style "D"

Early 1960's

$3 - $5

KAPP

KAPP RECORDS HAS

Roger Williams • Jane Morgan • Eartha Kitt • Four Lads • Carmen McRae • David Rose • The Hi-Lo's • Dimitri Tiomkin • Eddie Albert • Les Brown • Barbara Carroll • Bill Hayes • The Troubadors • Jose Jimenez • Pete King • Fred Astaire • Julius La Rosa • Ann Schein • Roger Voisin • Domenico Savino • John Gart • Kate Smith Carmichael • Amalia Rodrigues • Buddy Greco • Adele A' x • Vera Brynner • Larry Clinton • Clare Witkow lel & Aviva • Pete King • Jerry Keller • Bria Jack Elliott • Carlos Ramirez • Umberto e Morgan • Eartha Kitt • Four Lads • C e Hi-Lo's • Dimitri Tiomkin • Eddie Al • Bill Hayes • The Troubadors • Jose • Julius La Rosa • Ann Schein • Rog Gart • Kate Smith • Hoagy Carmichc eco • Adele Addison • Alan Lomax Clare Witkowski • The Delta Kings • Hi eller • Brian Hyland • Richard Wolfe • Jack erto Marcato • Roger Williams • Jane Morg ds • Carmen McRae • David Rose • The Hi-Lo's Eddie Albert • Les Brown • Barbara Carroll • Bill Hayes ubadors • Jose Jimenez • Pete King • Fred Astaire • Julius La Rosa • Ann Schein • Roger Voisin • Domenico Savino • John Gart • Kate Smith • Hoagy Carmichael • Amalia Rodrigues • Buddy Greco • Adele Addison • Alan Lomax • Vera Brynner • Larry Clinton • Clare Witkowski • The Delta Kings • Hillel & Aviva • Pete King • Jerry Keller • Brian Hyland • Richard Wolfe • Jack Elliott • Carlos Ramirez • Umberto Marcato • Roger Williams • Jane Morgan • Eartha Kitt • Four Lads • Carmen McRae • David Rose • The Hi-Lo's •

Back

Style "C"

Early 1960's

$4 - $6

KAPP

Front / Back

Style "E"

Mid 1960's

$3 - $5

KAPP

Front / Back
Style "F"
Mid 1960's
$3 - $5

KAPP

Front / Back
Style "H"
Mid – Late 1960's
$3 - $5

KAPP

Front / Back
Style "G"
Mid 1960's
$3 - $5

KAPP

Front / Back
Style "I"
Late 1960's
$3 - $5

KIRSHNER

Front / Back

Style "A"

Late 1960's

$2 - $4

KING

Front / Back

Style "A"

Early 1950's

$6 - $8

Different color combinations exist
and similarly valued (Except Green)

KIRSHNER

Front / Back

Style "B"

Late 1960's

$2 - $4

KING

Front / Back

Style "B"

Late 1950's

$10 - $12

K

KING

Front / Back
Style "C"
Early 1960's
$8 - $12

KING

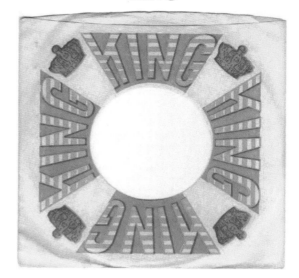

Front / Back
Style "E"
Late 1960's
$4 - $6

KING

Front / Back
Style "D"
Early – Mid 1960's
$4 - $6

LARKWOOD

Front (Back is plain)
Early 1960's
$8 - $10

LAURIE

Front / Back

1958 – 1969

$3 - $5

LIBERTY

Front / Back

Style "A"

Mid – Late 1950's

$8 - $10

LHI

Front / Back

Late 1960's

$3 - $5

LIBERTY

Front

Style "B"

Late 1950's

$10 - $12

LIBERTY

Back
Style "B"
Late 1950's
$10 - $12

LIBERTY

Front
Style "D"
Early 1960's
$3 - $5

LIBERTY

Front / Back
Style "C"
Early 1960's
$4 - $6

LIBERTY

Back
Style "D"
Early 1960's
$3 - $5

LIBERTY

Front / Back

Style "E"

Early – Mid 1960's

$4 - $6

White background

LIBERTY

Front / Back

Style "G"

Mid 1960's

$4 - $6

LIBERTY

Front / Back

Style "F"

Early – Mid 1960's

$4 - $6

Blue background

LIBERTY

Front / Back

Style "G"

Mid 1960's

$4 - $6

LIBERTY

Front / Back
Style "H"
Mid 1960's
$2 - $4

LIMELIGHT

Front / Back
Style "B"
Mid 1960's
$3 - $5

LIMELIGHT
Division of Mercury Records

Front / Back
Style "A"
Early – Mid 1960's
$3 - $5

LIMELIGHT

Front / Back
Style "C"
Late 1960's
$3 - $5

LOMA

Front / Back

Late 1960's

$3 - $5

LONDON

Front / Back

Style "B"

Late 1960's

$3 - $5

LONDON

(Printed in USA)

Front / Back

Style "A"

Early - Mid 1960's

$3 - $5

There are several paper and print color combinations similarly Valued.

M

Front / Back

Mid – Late 1960's

$2 - $4

M

MADISON

Front (back is plain)

Early 1960's

$4 - $6

There is a Madison sleeve that has
the same front and back which is
similarly valued.

MALA

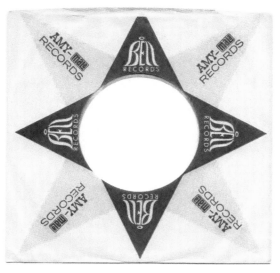

Front / Back

Style "B"

Mid – Late 1960's

$2 - $4

MALA

Front / Back

Style "A"

Early – Mid 1960's

$8 - $10

MAXWELL

Front / Back

Late 1960's

$2 - $4

MELODY

Motown Records

Front / Back

Mid 1960's

$6 - $8

MERCURY

Front / Back

Style "B"

Early 1950's

$6 - $8

Notice only one "45" showing at top. Also in white similarly valued.

MERCURY

Front / Back

Style "A"

Early 1950's

$6 - $8

MERCURY

Front

Style "C"

Mid 1950's

$3 - $5

MERCURY

Back

Style "C"

Mid 1950's

$3 - $5

This style also comes in blue
similarly valued.

MERCURY

Front / Back

Style "D"

Late 1950's

$3 - $5

MERCURY

Front / Back

Style "D"

Late 1950's

$3 - $5

MERCURY

Front / Back

Style "E"

Early 1960's

$3 - $5

MERCURY

Front / Back

Style "F"

Early 1960's

$3 - $5

MERCURY

Front

Style "H"

Late 1960's

$2 - $4

MERCURY

Front / Back

Style "G"

Early – Mid 1960's

$3 - $5

Red and black is similarly valued.

MERCURY

Back

Style "H"

Late 1960's

$2 - $4

MERCURY

Front / Back
Style "I"
Late 1960's
$2 - $4

MGM

Front
Style "A"
Early – Mid 1950's
$3 - $5

METRO
A Division of MGM

Front / Back
Late 1950's – Early 1960's
$6 - $8

MGM

Back
Style "A"
Early – Mid 1950's
$3 - $5

MGM

Front / Back

Style "B"

Late 1950's – Early 1960's

$3 - $5

White and yellow, similarly valued.

Blue is $6 - $8

MGM

Front / Back

Style "D"

Mid – Late 1960's

$3 - $5

MGM

Front / Back

Style "C"

Early 1960's

$6 - $8

MGM

Front / Back

Style "E"

Late 1960's

$2 - $4

M

MIAMI

Front (Plain back)
Early 1960's
$10 - $12

MIRANDA

Front / Back
Early – Mid 1960's
$8 - $10

MINIT

Front / Back
Early – Late 1960's
$3 - $5

MIRROR

Front / Back
Late 1960's
$6 - $8

MOD

Front / Back

Mid 1960's

$3 - $5

MODERN

Front / Back

Style "B"

Mid – Late 1950's

$6 - $8

MODERN

Front / Back

Style "A"

Early 1950's

$12 - $15

MODERN

Front / Back

Style "C"

Circa 1950's - 1960's

$6 - $8

Color variations exist, similarly valued.

MONUMENT

Front / Back
Style "A"
Late 1950's – Early 1960's
$6 - $8

MOSRITE

Front / Back
Late 1960's
$3 - $5

MONUMENT

Front / Back
Style "B"
Early – Late 1960's
$3 - $5

MOTIF

Front (Plain Back)
Late 1950's
$10 - $15

MOTOWN

Front / Back
Style "A"
Early 1960's
$10 - $15

MOTOWN

Front / Back
Style "B"
Mid 1960's
$6 - $8

MOTOWN

Front / Back
Style "B"
Early – Mid 1960's
$6 - $8

MOTOWN

Front & Back have many
variations
Style "D"
Mid – Late 1960's
$3 - $5

Many different color and print
variations exist, similarly valued.

MR. PEACOCK

Front (Plain Back)
Early 1960's
$10 - $12

MUSICLAND
Distributed by Bell Records

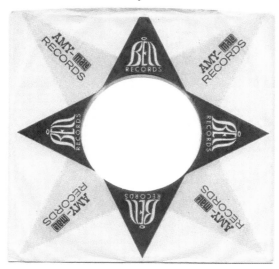

Front / Back
Mid 1960's
$2 - $4

MTA

Front / Back
Mid – Late 1960's
$10 - $15

MUSICOR
Distributed by United Artists

Front / Back
Style"A"
Early 1960's
$8 - $10

MUSICOR
Distributed by United Artists

Front / Back
Style "B"
Mid 1960's
$3 - $5

MUTUAL

Front / Back
Mid 1960's
$8 - $10

MUSICOR

Front / Back
Style "C"
Mid - Late 1960's
$3 - $5

NASCO
Distributed by Nashboro

Front / Back
Late 1960's
$3 - $5

NASHBORO

Front / Back

Style "A"

Late 1960's

$3 - $5

NATIONAL

Front / Back

Circa 1950's

$15 - $20

NASBORO

Front / Back

Style "B"

Late 1960's

$3 - $5

NATIONAL GENERAL

Front / Back

Late 1960's

$3 - $5

NEW VOICE
Distributed by Bell Records

Front / Back

Mid 1960's

$2 - $4

NRC
National Recording Company

Front / Back

Late 1950's – Early 1960's

$3 - $5

NEWTIME

Front / Back

Early 1960's

$8 - $10

NUGGET

Front / Back

Style "A"

Mid 1960's

$10 - $15

NUGGET

Front / Back

Style "B"

Late 1960's

$8 - $10

OKEH
Rhythm & Blues Sleeve

Front / Back – Style "A"

Early 1950's

$10- $15

ODE

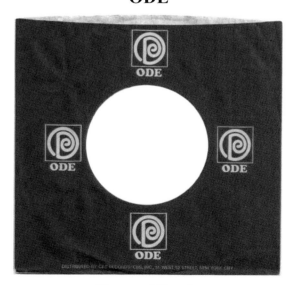

Front / Back

Late 1960's

$3- $5

OKEH

Front / Back – Style "B"

Circa 1950's

$6- $8

Color variations exist and are similarly valued. This design was used throughout the 1950's.

OKEH

Front / Back

Style "C"

Circa 1960's

$6- $8

Color variations exist and are
Similarly valued. This design was
used throughout the 1960's.

PACE

Front / Back

Mid – Late 1960's

$6 - $8

OLD TIMER

Front (Plain Back)

Early 1950's

$20 - $25

PACIFIC JAZZ

Front / Back

Mid – Late 1960's

$3 - $5

P

PAGE ONE
Distributed by Bell Records

Front / Back
Mid 1960's
$2 - $4

PARKWAY

Front / Back
Style "A"
Early 1960's
$8 - $10

PAGE ONE
Distributed by Bell Records

Front / Back
Late 1960's
$2 - $4

PARKWAY

Front / Back
Style "B"
Early - Mid 1960's
$4 - $6

PARKWAY

Front / Back

Style "C"

Mid – Late 1960's

$4 - $6

PARROT

A Division of London Records

Front / Back

Style "A"

Mid – Late 1960's

$4 - $6

PARKWAY

Front / Back

Style "D"

Late 1960's

$3 - $5

PARROT

Front / Back

Style "B"

Late 1960's

$3 - $5

PAULA RECORDS

Front / Back

Mid – Late 1960's

$6 - $8

PELHAM

Front / Back

Early 1960's

$6 - $8

PEACOCK

Front / Back

Late 1960's

$6 - $8

PETE

Front / Back

Late 1960's

$3 - $5

PHI DAN
A Division of Philles Records

Front / Back

Mid – Late 1960's

$6 - $8

PHILIPS
A Division of Mercury Records

Front / Back

Style "A"

Early - Mid 1960's

$3 - $5

Color Variations exist, similarly valued.

PHILIPS
A Division of Mercury Records

Front / Back

Style "B"

Late 1960's

$3 - $5

PHILIPS
A Division of Mercury Records

Front / Back

Style "C"

Late 1960's

$3 - $5

PHILLES

Front / Back

Mid – Late 1960's

$6 - $8

POMPEII

Front / Back

Late 1960's

$6 - $8

PLATO

Front (Plain Back)

Late 1960's

$20 - $25

POPPY

Front / Back

Late 1960's

$3 - $5

PREP

Front / Back

Late 1950's

$6 - $8

PRESS

Distributed by London Records

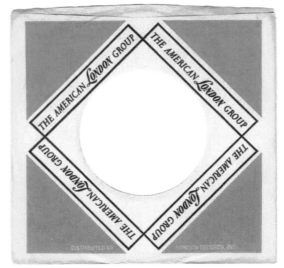

Front / Back

Mid 1960's

$3 - $5

Color variations exist, similarly valued.

PRIMA

Louis Prima's Record Company

Front / Back

Mid 1960's

$6 - $8

PROBE

A subsidiary of ABC Records

Front / Back

Late 1960's

$3 - $5

PULSAR
Distributed by Mercury Records

Front / Back
Late 1960's
$6 - $8

RAMA

Front / Back
Mid 1950's
$10 - $12

R-DELL (AARDELL)

Front / Back
Late 1950's Early 1960's
$6 - $8

RANWOOD

Front / Back
Late 1960's
$3 - $5

RCA VICTOR

Front / Back
Style "A"
1949 – Early 1950's
$4 - $6

RCA VICTOR

Front / Back
Style "C"
Early 1950's
$4 - $6

RCA VICTOR

Front / Back
Style "B"
Early 1950's
$4 - $6

RCA VICTOR

Front / Back
Style "D"
Mid 1950's
$4 - $6

RCA VICTOR

Front / Back

Style "E"

Mid – Late 1950's

$8 - $10

Color variations exist, similarly valued.

RCA VICTOR

Front / Back

Style "G"

Early - Mid 1960's

$3 - $5

Color variations exist, similarly valued.

RCA VICTOR

Front / Back

Style "F"

Late 1950's

$8 - $10

RCA VICTOR

Front / Back

Style "H"

Late 1960's

$3 - $5

RCA VICTOR

Front

Early 1950's

$6 - $8

REMEMBER

Front / Back

Late 1960's

$3 - $5

RCA VICTOR

Back

Early 1950's

$6 - $8

REMINGTON

Front / Back

Early – Mid 1950's

$6 - $8

RENDEZVOUS

Front / Back

Early 1960's

$6 - $8

REPRISE

Front / Back

Style "B"

Mid – Late 1960's

$3 - $5

REPRISE

Front / Back

Style "A"

Early – Mid 1960's

$3 - $5

Color variations exist, similarly valued.

REPRISE

Front / Back

Style "C"

Mid – Late 1960's

$3 - $5

REVUE

Front / Back

Mid – Late 1960's

$3 - $5

RONN

Front / Back

Mid – Late 1960's

$6 - $8

RIC

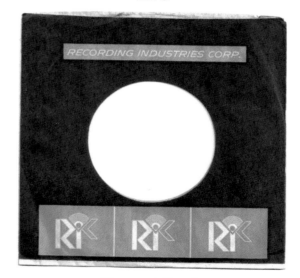

Front / Back

Mid – Late 1960's

$3 - $5

ROULETTE

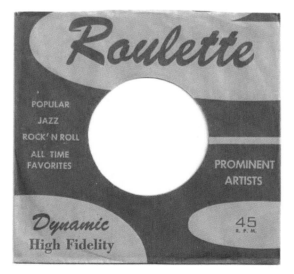

Front / Back

Style "A"

Late 1950's

$10 - $15

ROULETTE

Front / Back
Style "B"
Late 1950's
$6 - $8

ROULETTE

Front
Style "D"
Early - Mid 1960's
$3 - $5

ROULETTE

Front / Back
Style "C"
Early 1960's
$6 - $8

ROULETTE

Front
Style "D"
Early - Mid 1960's
$3 - $5

ROULETTE

Front
Style "E"
Early - Mid 1960's
$3 - $5

ROULETTE

Front / Back
Style "F"
Mid 1960's
$3 - $5

ROULETTE

Back
Style "E"
Early - Mid 1960's
$3 - $5

ROULETTE

Front / Back
Style "G"
Mid - Late 1960's
$3 - $5

Color variations exist, similarly valued.

RPM

Front / Back
Style "A"
Early 1950's
$20 - $25

SACRED

Front (Back is Plain)
Circa 1950's
$6 - $8

RPM

Front / Back
Style "B"
Circa 1950's - 1960's
$6 - $8

Color variations exist, similarly valued.

SCEPTER

Front Back
1960's
$6 $8

SEECO

Front
Style "A"
Circa 1950's
$10 - $15

SEECO

Front / Back
Late 1950's – Early 1960's
$6 - $8

SEECO

Back
Style "A"
Circa 1950's
$10 - $15

SENTAR (CENTAUR)
Distributed by Cameo Parkway

Front / Back
Mid – Late 1960's
$3 - $5

7 ARTS

Front / Back
Early 1960's
$10 - $15

SEVILLE
Distributed by London Records

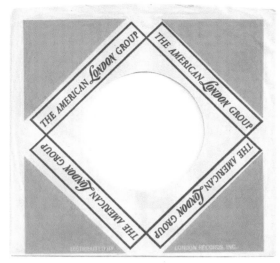

Front / Back
Style "B"
Mid 1960's
$3 - $5

SEVILLE

Front (Back is plain)
Style "A"
Late 1950's - Early 1960's
$8 - $10

SGC
Distributed by Atlantic – Atco

Front / Back
Style "A"
1965 – 1969
$3 - $5

SHOW TOWN

Front / Back

1969

$10 - $15

SIGNATURE

Front (Back is plain)

Style "A"

Circa 1960's

$6 - $8

SIDEWALK

Front / Back

Mid – Late 1960's

$8 - $10

SIGNATURE

Front

Style "B"

Circa 1960's

$6 - $8

SIGNATURE

Back
Style "B"
Circa 1960's
$6 - $8

SILVER SPOTLIGHT SERIES
Distributed by United Artists

Front / Back
Mid – Late 1960's
$3 - $5

SILVER
Distributed By Allied Record

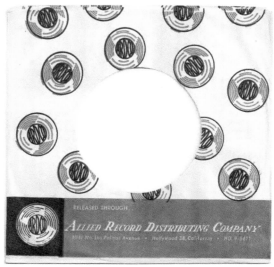

Front / Back
Circa 1960
$8 - $10

SINGSPIRATION

Front / Back
Circa 1950's
$6 - $8

SIRE
Distributed by London Records

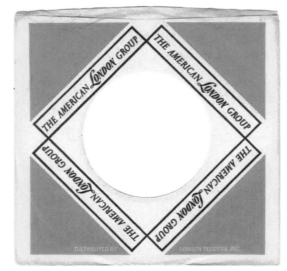

Front / Back

Mid 1960's

$3 - $5

SMASH

Front / Back

Style "B"

Late 1960's

$3 - $5

SMASH

Front / Back

Style "A"

Early – Late 1960's

$3 - $5

SOLID STATE

Front / Back

Late 1960's

$3 - $5

S

SOLO

Front / Back
Circa Mid 1950's
$15 - $20

SONG HITS

Front / Back
Circa Early – Mid 1960's
$8 - $10

Color variations exist, similarly valued.

SOMA

Front / Back
Circa 1960's
$3 - $5

SOUL

Front / Back
Mid 1960's
$6 - $8

SOUND

Front / Back

Mid 1960's

$8 - $10

SPECIALTY

Front (Back is plain)

Late 1950's – 1960's

$8 - $10

SOUND STAGE 7

Front / Back

Circa 1963 – 1969

$3 - $5

SPRING

Front / Back

Circa 1969

$3 - $5

S

STACY

Front / Back
Circa 1959 – 1964
$15 - $20

STARDAY

Front / Back
Style "B"
Mid 1960's
$4 - $6

STARDAY

Front / Back
Style "A"
Early – Mid 1960's
$4 - $6

STARDAY

Front / Back
Style "C"
Late 1960's
$3 - $5

STAX

Front / Back

Mid – Late 1960's

$3 - $5

STRAND

Front / Back

Early 1960's

$6 - $8

STEED

Front / Back

Late 1960's

$8 - $10

SUN

Front / Back

Circa 1950's – 1960's

$4 - $6

SURF

Front (Back is plain)
Late 1950's
$10 - $15

TAMLA

Front / Back
Early – Mid 1960's
$10 - $15

SWING TIME

Front / Back
Circa 1950's
$10 - $15

TETRAGRAMMATON

Front / Back
Late 1960's
$8 - $10

TODAY'S HITS

Front / Back
Early 1960's
$8 - $10

TOP RANK

Front / Back
Circa 1959 – 1961
$8 - $10

TOGETHER

Front / Back
Circa 1969
$4 - $6

TOWER

Front / Back
Early – Late 1960's
$4 - $6

TRX

Front / Back
Late 1960's
$4 - $6

UNI

Front / Back
Late 1960's
$3 - $5

UNART
Division of United Artists

Front (Back is plain)
Circa 1958
$10 - $15

UNICAL RECORDS

Front / Back
Early 1960's
$8 - $10

UNIQUE

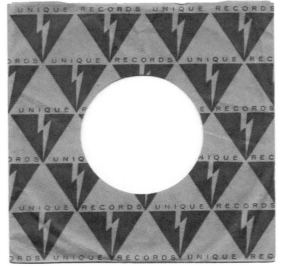

Front / Back
Mid 1950's
$15 - $20

UNITED ARTISTS

Front / Back
Style "B"
Early 1960's
$6 - $8

UNITED ARTISTS

Front (Back is plain)
Style "A"
Circa 1950's
$10 - $15

UNITED ARTISTS

Front
Style "C"
Early 1960's
$3 - $5

UNITED ARTISTS

Back
Style "C"
Early 1960's
$3 - $5

UNITED ARTISTS

Back
Style "D"
Early 1960's
$3 - $5

UNITED ARTISTS

Front
Style "D"
Early 1960's
$3 - $5

UNITED ARTISTS

Front
Style "E"
Early 1960's
$3 - $5

UNITED ARTISTS

Back

Style "E"

Early 1960's

$3 - $5

Other similar sleeves exist with different photos and layouts, similarly valued.

UNITED ARTISTS

Front / Back

Style "F"

Early 1960's

$4 - $6

UNITED ARTISTS

Front / Back

Style "G"

Mid - Late 1960's

$3 - $5

This sleeve also comes in several different colors, all similarly valued.

UNITED ARTISTS

Front / Back

Style "H"

Late 1960's

$3 - $5

UNITED ARTISTS JAZZ

Front / Back
Circa 1962
$10 - $15

VARSITY

Front / Back
Circa 1950's
$6 - $8

USA

Front / Back
Mid – Late 1960's
$6 - $8

VEE JAY

Front / Back
Early – Mid 1960's
$6 - $8

VEE JAY

Front / Back

Mid 1960's

$6 - $8

VERVE

Front / Back

Late 1950's – Early 1960's

$8 - $12

VEEP
A Division of United Artists

Front / Back

Mid – Late 1960's

$8 - $12

VIK

Front / Back

Late 1950's

$8 - $12

VIM

Front / Back
Circa 1959/60
$8 - $12

VMC

Front / Back
Late 1960's
$8 - $12

VIVA

Front / Back
Mid – Late 1960's
$3 - $5

WAND

Front / Back
1960's
$4 - $6

WARNER BROS.

Front / Back

Late 1950's

$8 - $12

WARNER BROS.

Front / Back

Late 1950's

$20 - $25

This is a library index sleeve.

WARNER BROS.

Front / Back

Late 1950's

$10 - $15

WARNER BROS.

Front / Back

Late 1950's – Early 1960's

$6 - $8

WARNER BROS.

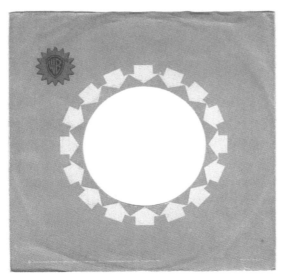

Front / Back
Early – Mid 1960's
$3 - $5

WARNER BROS.

Front / Back
Late 1960's
$2 - $4

WARNER BROS.

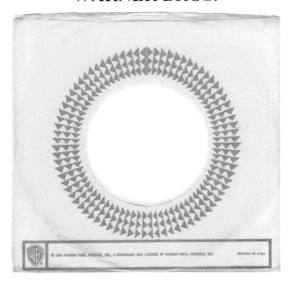

Front / Back
Mid – Late 1960's
$3 - $5

WARWICK

Front / Back
Late 1950's – Early 1960's
$6 - $8

WE MAKE ROCK "N ROLL RECORDS
MFG by Capitol Records

Front / Back

1968

$6 - $8

WHITE WHALE

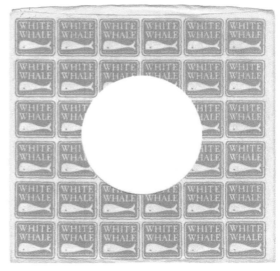

Front / Back

Mid – Late 1960's

$4 - $6

WEB

Front / Back

Circa 1950's

$25 - $30

WINDSOR

Front / Back

Circa Early 1960's

$4 - $6

WING
Subsidiary of Mercury Records

Front
Circa 1955
$6 - $8

WINRO

Front / Back
Circa 1969
$4 - $6

WING

Back
Circa 1955
$6 - $8

WORLD ARTISTS

Front / Back
Style "A"
Mid 1960's
$6 - $8

WORLD ARTISTS

Front / Back
Style "B"
Mid 1960's
$3 - $5

WORLD PACIFIC JAZZ

Front / Back
Late 1960's
$3 - $5

WORLD PACIFIC

Front / Back
Mid 1960's
$6 - $8

Color variations exist, similarly
valued

WYE

Front / Back
Circa 1960
$20 - $25

"X"

Front / Back

Mid 1950's

$6 - $8

Also comes with Red "X" on sleeve.

Sleeve Index

Made in the USA
Columbia, SC
03 February 2021